IMAGINE THAT

Licensed exclusively to Imagine That Publishing Ltd
Tide Mill Way, Woodbridge, Suffolk, IP12 1AP, UK
www.imaginethat.com
Copyright © 2020 Imagine That Group Ltd
All rights reserved
2 4 6 8 9 7 5 3 1
Manufactured in China

Written by Jemima Summer
Illustrated by P.S. Brooks

ISBN 978-1-78958-306-9

A catalogue record for this book is available from the British Library

The Last Unicorn

Written by Jemima Summer
Illustrated by P.S. Brooks

Little Unicorn was the last unicorn in the whole wide world. More than anything, she wished for a unicorn friend to prance, play and neigh with.

One day, Little Unicorn was feeling sad and lonely.

As she walked through a magical wood, Little Unicorn imagined the fun games that she could play with other unicorns.

As tears filled Little Unicorn's eyes, a tiny fairy landed on a branch beside her.

'What's the matter, Little Unicorn?' asked the tiny fairy, kindly.

'I'm the last unicorn in the whole wide world and I have no one to prance, play and neigh with!' she sobbed.

'Please don't cry,' said the tiny fairy.

'I'm sure I saw something with a horn just like yours by the magical fairy tree. Perhaps it's another unicorn – follow me!'

Little Unicorn trotted after the tiny fairy
and before long they heard a clippety-clop of hooves.

*Maybe I'm not the last unicorn in the whole wide world
after all,* thought Little Unicorn excitedly.

The sound of hooves stopped as they reached the magical fairy tree and a head with long horns poked up through the bushes.

But it wasn't a unicorn at all. It was a goat!

'You've got too many horns to be a unicorn!' said Little Unicorn disappointedly.

'You're right,' said the goat, 'but I did see something with only one horn by the magic toadstool ring up ahead!'

Little Unicorn thanked the goat, and together they set off towards
the magic toadstool ring with the tiny fairy.

After a short canter, Little Unicorn heard a loud drumming of hooves. In the distance, she spotted something with a single horn charging towards them.

Maybe I'm not the last unicorn in the whole wide world after all, thought Little Unicorn excitedly.

But it wasn't a unicorn at all. It was a rhino!

'You're not graceful enough to be a unicorn!' said Little Unicorn disappointedly.

'You're right,' said the rhino, 'but I did see something with one horn down at the mermaid pool. It was graceful, too!'

Little Unicorn thanked the rhino, and together they set off towar the mermaid pool with the tiny fairy and the goat.

After a short gallop, Little Unicorn heard the sound of falling water. As she reached the mermaid pool, a single, long horn cut gracefully through the water.

Maybe I'm not the last unicorn in the whole wide world after all,
thought Little Unicorn excitedly.

But it wasn't a unicorn at all. It was a narwhal!

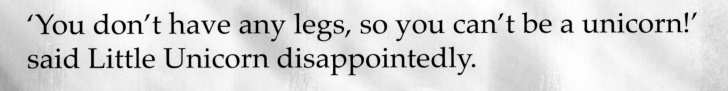

'You don't have any legs, so you can't be a unicorn!'
said Little Unicorn disappointedly.

'You're right,' said the narwhal, 'but I'm graceful and
I have a long horn, just like you.'

Tears filled Little Unicorn's eyes again.

'I'm the last unicorn in the whole wide world and I have no one to prance, play and neigh with!' she sobbed.

Then Little Unicorn remembered how kind the tiny fairy, the goat, the rhino and the narwhal had been to her when she was looking for a unicorn friend.

'Will you be my friends and prance, play and neigh with me?' asked Little Unicorn.

'Yes!' replied Little Unicorn's new friends all at once.

Little Unicorn and her friends played happily ever after.